To Holly and Emily
Happy Easter with Love from Shirley, James.
xx Co

The Easter Bunny invites
you on an
Easter Adventure

an Easter Adventure

The
Easter Bunny
comes to
Scotland

GRACE   JACK

Written by Lily Jacobs
Illustrated by Robert Dunn and Darran Holmes
Designed by Sarah Allen

First published by HOMETOWN WORLD in 2016
Hometown World Ltd
7 Northumberland Buildings
Bath BA1 2JB

www.hometownworld.co.uk

ISBN 978-1-78553-232-0

10 9 8 7 6 5 4 3 2 1

an Easter Adventure

The Easter Bunny comes to Scotland

Written by Lily Jacobs
Illustrated by Robert Dunn

CHILDHOOD DREAMS
HOMETOWN WORLD

Our story begins in a wonderful place
With a boy named Jack and a girl named Grace.

WELCOME TO
SCOTLAND

JOHN
O'GROATS
2040

LANDS END 874

PENTLAND SKERRIES 6

ORKNEY &
SHETLAND ISLES

YOUR TOWN

They were moving to Scotland and longed to explore,
Make friends, have adventures and many things more!

Scotland Pet Store

On the day before Easter,
they drove into town.
They went to the pet store
and looked all around.

There in the front
was a pen full of bunnies.
The small ones were cute.
The big ones were funny!

They played with the bunnies
and thought for a bit,
And then they agreed
on the most *perfect* fit:

The *littlest* bunny,
with a floppity-hop.

"He's the one!" they decided.
"Let's call him Flop."

So Flop joined the family
that sunny spring day.
The littlest bunny
was now home to stay.

They played until bedtime, then made a snug nest,
And settled Flop into his cage for a rest.

Grace gave Flop a kiss.
Jack patted his head,
Then the two happy children
climbed into bed.

A soft evening breeze blew in through the window,
As Grace and Jack fell fast asleep on their pillows.

But Flop had no time now
to close his own eyes –
He was preparing
an Easter surprise!

Although he was small,
(and he knew it was true)
Tonight little Flop
had a big job to do.

For he had a secret
he hadn't let show:

He was the Easter Bunny,
and he had to go!

A magical wind gave his whiskers a tickle.
His nose, how it twitched! His ears, how they wiggled!

Soon, Flop was quite different from ever before,
And he couldn't wait – not for one moment more!

He raced through the house and out into the night,
To where he had hidden his eggs out of sight.

His marvellous burrow held Easter eggs plenty:
To be quite exact, **nine million and twenty!**
He packed up the eggs. He looked at the map.
He fastened his goggles and his flying cap.

Then Flop hopped right into
his hot air balloon.
And soon he was soaring
as high as the moon!

As he watched his first stop grow nearer and nearer,
His big Scotland mission became even clearer.

First, Flop balanced eggs
on a tall building top...

...Then, went to
the park, spreading
eggs as he hopped.

He kicked a fine goal
(just for some fun...)

...And quietly hid
chocolate eggs,
one by one.

With big bounces here and giant jumps there,

Flop hid Scotland's eggs everywhere!

WEST   EAST

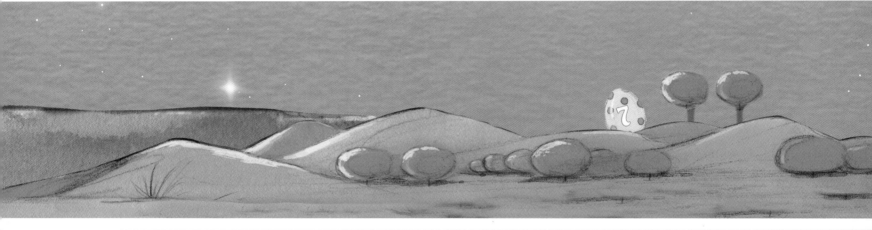

He flew to the **east**, to the **south**, **west** and **north**.
He crisscrossed the country, he raced **back** and **forth**.

Edinburgh, Stirling and Thurso got treats,
Then Aberdeen, Dumfries and Fife were complete.

Kilmarnock, Dundee – the long list went on.

Flop was delivering eggs until dawn!

Finally, Flop found his very last stop.
He came to **your** house with a bounce and a hop!
And there he delivered his Easter surprises –
Chocolate eggs, of all shapes and sizes!
And when he had finished,
he stopped for a rest.

16

Yes, surely this Easter
was one of his best!

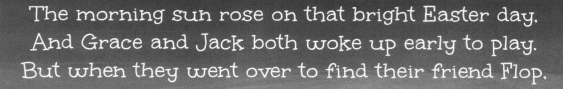

The morning sun rose on that bright Easter day,
And Grace and Jack both woke up early to play.
But when they went over to find their friend Flop,

The door was wide open —
his cage was unlocked!

There were eggs to discover for Grace and for Jack.
But now Flop was **missing**,
they just wanted him back!

They looked under their beds. They looked all around.
But their new bunny friend just couldn't be found.

But, whose goggles were these?

Who unfolded this map?

Then from the garden came a faint *tap-tap-tap*.
They rushed and they stumbled. It had to be him!
And there they found baskets —
with something tucked in!

"It's Flop!" they cried out, and they held him so close.
Jack tickled his ears. Grace kissed his pink nose.
Flop hugged the two children, his new friends so dear.

Happy Easter to Scotland!
See you next year!

Did you find all the Easter eggs
hidden in Scotland?
Look back through the book to see
if you can spot all 20 eggs.

Give up?
Check the answers
on the last page.